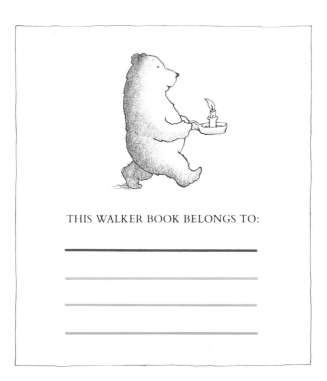

THIS WALKER BOOK BELONGS TO:

_____

_____

_____

_____

First published 1987 by
Walker Books Ltd
87 Vauxhall Walk
London SE11 5HJ

© 1987 Jan Ormerod

This edition published 1990

Printed and bound in Italy by L.E.G.O., Vicenza

British Library Cataloguing in Publication Data
Ormerod, Jan
Bend and stretch.—(New baby books).
I. Title   II. Series
823[J]   PZ7
ISBN 0-7445-1492-4

Bend and Stretch

Jan Ormerod

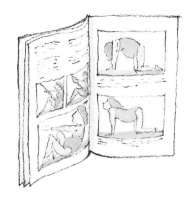

WALKER BOOKS
LONDON

Breathe in and up.

Breathe out and down.

Left leg, right leg,
round and round.

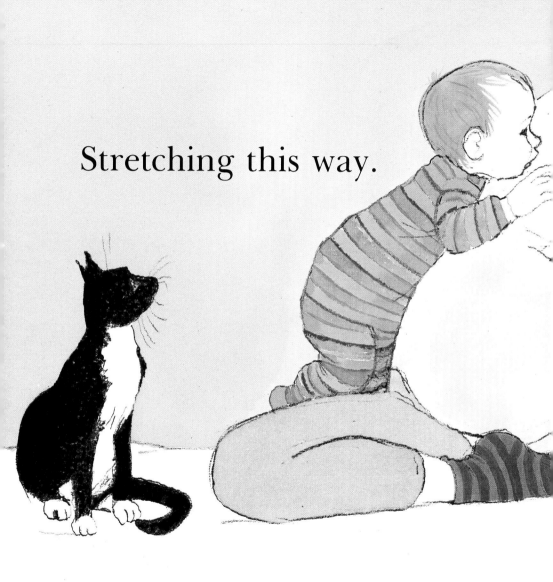

Stretching this way.

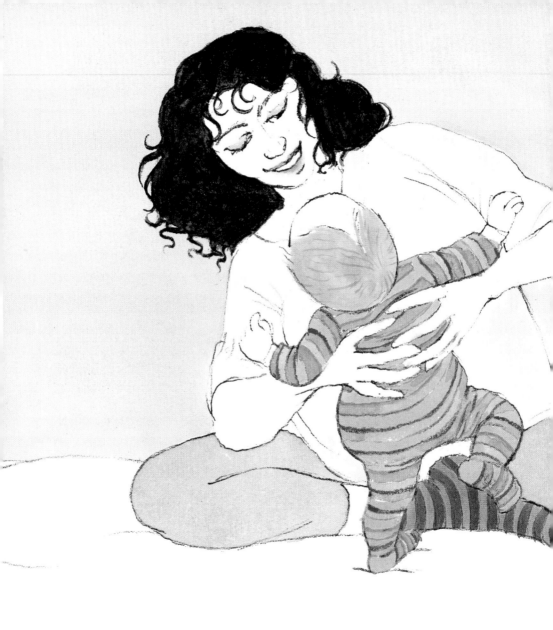

Stretching that way.

In, out,
    up, down,
        round and round.

Tickle, tickle, tickle.
Giggle, giggle, giggle.

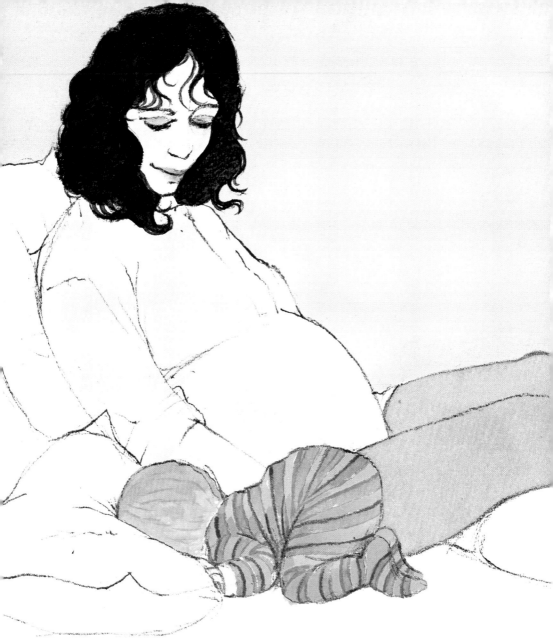

Rest and relax.

MORE WALKER PAPERBACKS
For You to Enjoy

Also by Jan Ormerod
DAD AND ME
"Gentle, humorous and true to life." *TES*

ISBN 0-7445-0927-0   READING
ISBN 0-7445-0928-9   SLEEPING
ISBN 0-7445-0929-7   MESSY BABY
ISBN 0-7445-0930-0   DAD'S BACK
£1.99 each

LITTLE ONES
"Refreshingly unsentimental." *British Book News*

ISBN 0-7445-1342-1   OUR OLLIE
ISBN 0-7445-1344-8   SILLY GOOSE
ISBN 0-7445-1345-6   JUST LIKE ME
£1.99 each